Clint Faraday
book fifty three
Dead Serious

Clint is visiting friends in Santiago when a man from Brazil says he is going to stand up to the local excuse for a mafia.

A local lawyer says, "You can't be serious!"

"Dead serious," he replies.

Then the bodies start showing up. They are the bodies of the man's associates and friends.

Is the mafia eliminating problems before they start? Then why not kill Sargento?

Clint doesn't think so.

Contents

About the Author

CD Moulton has traveled extensively over much of the world both in the music business, where he was a rock guitarist, songwriter, and arranger, and in an import/export business. He has been everything from a bar owner to auto salvage (junkyard) manager, longshoreman to high steel worker, orchid grower to landscaper, tropical fish farmer to commercial fisherman. He started writing books in 1983 and has published more than 125 books as of January 1, 2012. His most popular books to date are about research with orchids, though much of his science fiction and fantasy work has proven popular. He wrote the CD Grimes, PI series and the Det. Nick Storie series, among other works.

He now resides in David, Panamá, where he writes the Clint Faraday mystery series, plays music with friends – and pursues his favorite ways to spend his time: beach bum and roaming the mountains doing botanical research. He has recently become involved in fighting the corruption that is rampant in the legal and judicial system. "I love Panama' and that is hurting this country badly."

CD is involved in research of natural cancer cure at this time. It has proven effective in all cases, so far. It is based on a plant that has been in use for thousands of years, is safe, available, and cheap. He has studied botany, and was cured of a serious lymphoma with use of the plant, *Ambrosia peruviana*.

Information about this cure is free on the FaceBook page, Ambrosia peruviana for cancer. CD asks only that all who try it please report on its effectiveness on that group.

<u>*A Nice Lunch*</u>

Clint Faraday, retired PI from Florida, now living in Panamá, talked with a couple of his Indigeno friends in the little park in Santiago. He caught them up with what was going on in the comarca (Indigeno land) and they caught him up on what was happening in Santiago.

To tell the truth, very little was new. It was a laid-back time. The same scams perpetrated by the same people on the same people. The faces and names changed on the victim end, but they were the same. Mostly retired people who were subject to lose their life's savings to the crooks the government seemed very reluctant to stop. It was killing a lot of investment in Panamá, sad as it was.

A man from Brazil who Clint met the night before, Carlos Sargento, came to talk with them. He seemed a good enough person, a little naive, perhaps, but an amiable and open enough guy.

They went to the small restaurant near the bus terminal for a very nice little lunch. Santos and Emilio, Clint's Indio friends, joined Sargento and Willam Juarez and Charlie Andrews, friends of

Carlos. They had their favorite comida corriente, Clint choosing the carne aguisado and peach nectar for the beverage. They discussed Clint's homes in Quebrada Tula and Cusapín, both on the Ngobe Bugle comarca. (Clint was honored to be the second white person to be declared Ngobe by the council. His beautiful wife was a Ngobe and his two young children were being raised in the Indio tradition, which Clint found far superior to the Latin or gringo cultures.)

Another man came to join them, Jorge Andros, also from Brazil. He said he was butting his head on a fence post to try to get any action from this crooked, corrupt court system.

He was like Clint's friend, Dave, in that he had been scammed out of some property. There was a fifty-fifty chance he could get it back after a few years of fighting the system, but he was resigned to the probability that those slimewads would get away with it – again.

"It's the same ones. I found there are more than thirty denunciados against them, but the fiscalia refuses to even investigate them. Been paid off or scared of them. It's enough to make you want to lead a revolution here," Jorge complained. "We should talk of more pleasant things, I think."

"I don't have anything happening in my life right now. I think I'll go after those so-called amateur mafia thugs," Carlos said with a wry grin. "I have a few connections. Maybe I can find a little excitement. I'm mostly bored. I came to try to get the system to act, but that's hopeless.

"They might be scared of those hoods, but I'm not! I'm sixty four and have led a good life. They kill me, no loss to the world. Maybe I can take a few of them with me!"

"Fight them directly? You can't be serious!" Jorge declared. "You'd need an army! There's one of you or maybe five of us, but there are fifty five of them! They could come after us ten for one!

"You can't be serious!"

"Dead serious," Carlos answered. "I can go after them one at the time. They won't know where I'm coming from. They don't know me. No one here does except us few here. Everyone knows who they are and where they are! One at the time. Two months, they aren't any more.

"That's if I can survive that long, of course."

"I'm in!" Charlie said, grinning. "Hell, I'm just a fugitive from Oregon who's living in Brazil and visiting here. I have to admit I'm qualified in ... certain ways."

"This is totally crazy!" Willam declared. "Count me in!"

Clint said he would do what he could, but in an indirect way. He worked with the police and knew the problem was mostly from the corrupt court system. Most of the police, particularly the PTJ, did their job, then the courts refused to act against certain people. Santo and Emilio said they could get information. After all, they were just a couple of Indio workers no one would even notice.

Clint had heard a lot of people who said they'd fight the corruption, but damned few of them even made a move. He figured this was more of the same crap. They were actually going to make plans, but that would be where it ended. Too many of the hoods had come up through the drug cartels and were brutal and dangerous.

"You have families?" Carlos asked.

"I have a wife and two kids," Clint answered. "They can't get to them on the comarca."

"Emilio and I have some family, but they are on the comarca, too," Santo replied.

"You stay out of it. Maybe you can find some information – but only if who you are won't be known," Carlos warned sternly. "This isn't your fight. It's ours."

"It's mine," Jorge said. "I should fight it, but we're soldiers of fortune by psychology, so it will be fun!"

"You're totally loco! So are we. Let's get it on!" Willam said.

They slapped palms all around, then changed the

subject. Later in the afternoon Clint drove on to David. He would return to his home and family in Quebrada Tula where they didn't have those kind of hoods to contend with.

Clint liked going to the cities less and less – and he started with that being very low on his list of priorities. He had to go back to Santiago for the council in two weeks. He didn't care to hear anything about this again. He suspected it was all talk and over before it began anyhow.

It was a very long way from the first time he suspected wrong.

<u>*Phone Messages*</u>

Clint was back home for three days when he got a call from Santo. It seemed Willam Juarez from their lunch in Santiago was found dead. Killed execution-style.

"Clint, I think Carlos is really doing something and those crooks think it was Willam. Milio and I were asked some questions by the man at the fiscalia. He asked what we knew of those Brazil people. It was, as he said, 'noted' that we had lunch with them. We said it was all about the economy of Brazil and Panamá and we didn't know anything about that – or care.

"Flaco Perez was hit by a car yesterday early in the morning. They don't know why he was out on the carretera. The car that hit him was maybe the one Willam was driving, but maybe not.

"You know who Flaco was. The mafia man who collected the money they said people owed them. People with almacens and kioscos. People who didn't owe them anything. It was maybe them, not Willam, who hit the piece of shit."

"I think I have Carlos' number. I'll see what he knows. Be careful."

They chatted a minute more, then Clint called Carlos, who said Willam had talked too much in the wrong places. He didn't know – for certain – Willam had hit the SOB, but he probably did.

"Some cop was asking Santos and Emilio about the lunch meeting. They said we talked about the economy, which they didn't know or care anything about.

"Let out that involving the Indios in anything will result in me taking action. They know what that can mean."

He soon rang off and sat back to think. This had better not get out of hand. It damned well better not involve the Indios, who had nothing to do with anything.

Nito, his ten year old son, came in to say his daughter, Nicole, and wife, Tyna, were going to be in town for the day so he would work with Lino in the yampi. They had an order for a lot from David. A new restaurant that was going to feature pollo Panameño with yampi and otoe. Clint was going to be working on building a water tank for the town in the mountains where the drop in altitude would give them very good pressure. He had designed the system, complete with filters. The pressure meant the water would go through a form of RO that would guarantee no parasites or bacteria would get through.

Clint had millions of dollars from his cases that he spent on building schools and clinics on the comarca for those he considered as his people. He was working in the fields and fishing and whatever was needed, the same as the others. He was thoroughly enjoying the life of the Indios, which was rewarding. It left him with a strong sense of belonging and of accomplishment, which he'd never known before adopting the lifestyle.

His children were being raised in the tradition. They had a place and a purpose. They had their own responsibilities since before they were six years old. They belonged and knew it, which Clint never knew in the 54 years before he came to the comarca.

He smiled. He felt *good* here! The physical labor had him in great condition. He was 70 years old and the gringos he met all thought he was in his late forties at most. He didn't have the normal aches and pains a man of his age had in cities and particularly in the states or Europe. Dave, his nutty musician/botanist friend, was over eighty and still tramped around through the mountains where no white man had ever gone before like he did when he first started the research here. He was 68 years old, then and would leave most of the younger city people behind before an hour was out.

He was the one who had his entire retirement stolen by these half-baked mafia characters. He'd been fighting them for more than nine years and had made very little progress.

Clint was glad to see a few of them knocked off. It was part of what they knew the moment they went into the mobs, that they were at risk. He hoped the courts would pursue whoever was knocking them off with exactly the same vigor they displayed in prosecuting for their victims.

He sighed, picked up his backpack with the tools and headed for the water project.

"Clint? Emilio here. Santo said he called you about Willam. There are two more of the thugs dead. They fell off that cliff by the river toward Veraguas. A sad accident – and why were they anywhere near there?

"This policia capitan for the fiscalia, Arturo Ramos, keeps asking Santo and me about what Carlos and his friends were talking about. We tell them we don't listen to that economy talk. It doesn't mean anything to us.

"Ramos is very nervous. Why?"

"Because he sees himself about to be charged with corruption, probably. If that bunch doesn't go into hiding, someone's going to be caught and taken to Panamá City. He'll run his mouth to save his own rotten hide, which means testifying against the corrupt people in the courts here, which means he's the one in position to be the goat."

"The goat? I don't ... oh! The one who gets the blame so the bigger ones aren't mentioned?"

"Uh-huh. Be careful. If it gets worse, I'll come. They should have been warned not to bother my people. You have nothing to do with either side there."

"If he asks again, I'll call you. Maybe you can talk to him."

"Done!"

They chatted a few more minutes. Clint went back to the house where Tyna had a delicious lobster stew prepared for dinner. Nito and Nicole told him about their day, he told about his, Tyna told about hers. They went to the stream to bathe (they had a shower in the house, but preferred the stream) before sitting on the porch to watch the spectacular sunset, then went to the house for the kids to do their homework. They went to school five days and worked one. Sunday or Wednesday meant nothing on the comarca away from the outside cities.

Silvio, the chief of the local area, came to chat and ask that Clint go to Buabidi to see what the problem was with the museum (Clint had been instrumental in establishing a museum around a pirate ship. Book 51: *Dead Man Talking*) and some people from Spain, who wanted to claim the treasure was theirs. Clint could probably inform them they stood no chance of getting a centavo in a more diplomatic way than he would.

Clint agreed. He would go in the morning. He had the helicopter that could deliver him in little time.

It would cost him more than a thousand dollars for the round trip, but what the hell? He didn't have much other use for his money.

He didn't think much more about Santiago. That would probably resolve itself, one way or another.

Santo called back at about ten o'clock to say he would appreciate it if Clint would tell Capitan Ramos what they talked about with that Carlos person. The one from Argentina or Brazil or wherever.

"Capitan Ramos? Clint Faraday here. What the hell's going on? Why do you keep molesting my friends about having lunch with me and some people I met in the park?"

"Er, those people are suspected of, er, bringing in drugs. They may have said something that we could, uh, you know."

"No. I don't know. What's really going on? There are no drugs coming into Santiago except a little coke and some marijuana, same as always. The Indios don't use either. No more shit. What's it about?"

"It seems, well, that there are several dead people in a group who are – dangerous. They want to know who is killing them. It is possible the people from Brazil are part of that. We have to stop ... that is, we can't have ... you see what I mean."

"You mean that someone is knocking off a few of your local excuses for excuses of a mafia and you could get your dirty ass in a serious crack if anyone there decides to throw you to the system to protect themselves. You knew that was the deal when you got into it. Don't cry about it when it happens.

"Leave my friends out of it. The Indios don't even know what it's about. All we talked about at that lunch meeting was about how Brazil and Panamá were the only two places in the Americas with strong economies. They couldn't care less about economies.

"Tell your hood friends that, one more time and I come there. They don't want that. You damned well don't

"Clear?"

"Er."

Clint rang off and swore.

Well, tomorrow Buabidi. Maybe he would go to Santiago. He damned well would if they didn't leave his friends out of their private little war.

He played and teased with Tyna and the kids, then went to bed.

"... say that the treasure was on your ships so it belongs to you, to Spain.

"Got some news for you! That was stolen from the people of Colombia. You are admitting that it was sponsored by Spain? The theft and rape of the cultures here? You claim that Spain wants that stolen treasure delivered to them now? Is that your argument?"

"Of course not! It was gold and jewels that we had paid for!"

"Paid for the killing a lot of the natives to take their gold? *That* is the argument? That Spain *paid* those pirates to kill the natives and steal their gold, so it's yours?"

"No! We didn't say any such thing!"

"Then you can repeat what you did say for the record. We can see where it's any different than that."

The panel of seven international lawyers and a fat diplomat from Spain went into an animated discussion among themselves. Silvio grinned at Clint and gave him a thumb up.

Finally the diplomat, Modesto, said they would handle it through the courts in Panamá City.

"Those Panamanian courts have no authority on the comarca," Basilio, acting chief, said sternly. "You deal with us. No technicalities and no deals where you pay some corrupt judge to find in your favor. I am the law here as well as the court.

"Do you wish to present any further argument before I give a decision?"

"We will find more evidence while you ponder the question and will present it before you hand down the decision," the diplomat said.

"What's there to ponder?" Basilio asked. "You are here to claim ownership of articles because you paid somebody to steal them and they were then stolen from your murderers and thieves. Court finds you have no case, that this was a silly, frivolous bringing. If you continue this, you will pay the court costs."

"No! Our client will meet with your diplomatic department to present the case more clearly and in terms that are recognized by the world legal system," a lawyer replied haughtily.

"I am also the diplomatic department who has appointed Clinton Faraday to handle that end of things," Basilio warned. "This is the comarca. This is not a corrupt court like you are used to bribing to get what you might want.

"Is this to announce that you wish to continue this frivolity?"

"*Frivolity?!* We are talking about billions of Balboas in treasure! *That* is hardly frivolous!" a lawyer cried.

"We are talking about billions of Balboas in treasure that you have admitted you paid others to kill for and steal. Perhaps Clint can explain in more diplomatic language what I have ruled."

"Mr. Faraday, perhaps we can come to a decision that is fair to everyone?" the diplomat suggested. "I am sure you can understand what this means to Spain in this horrible time of world recession."

"That you want to bring the recession to the comarca by stealing the treasure again?" Clint asked innocently.

"Of course not! That's a terrible thing to say!"

"But true," Basilio countered. "If there is nothing more? I want to view the route of the new road to the CPA."

"We need your decision as soon as it can be tendered!" a lawyer shouted.

"What? You're stupid? I tendered my decision. This is a frivolous case and is dismissed. That's it! Case closed, or whatever you say."

"Your honor, if I may ask a question?" a man sitting in one of the few chairs asked.

"Yes? I'm Basilio. I'm not 'Your honor' or any

of that silliness."

"I'm with United Free Press International. I understand that your word is absolute law on the comarca. I wish to ask if there is an appeals system here?"

"No. They can continue the case if they think they can make any difference with new evidence, but that will be at their expense."

"We'll do that!" the diplomat said with a sneer.

"Very well. Court costs will be one billion Balboas per day. I will hear your arguments in fifteen days. That will leave us owing you fifteen billion if you change my mind or you owing us fifteen billion when I declare it's still frivolous.

"I warn you now that better evidence than some old records that show you paid privateers to kill my people and steal their gold will be required."

They looked around at each other, then walked out – except the diplomat, who wanted a word with the reporter.

"I'm Adam Claberg. You don't have anything to say to me that you would not wish to appear in the press I take it?"

He looked uncertain, then he walked out.

"What a gaggle of clowns!" Claberg said. "Can I buy you all a beer?"

"Sounds like a reasonable plan," Clint replied. "Balboa, please."

They went out of the council room laughing and joking about the case. The diplomat was standing beside a ridiculously long limousine talking to some reporters. One of them saw Clint and called that he had a question or two. The diplomat looked like he would explode.

"How about I tell you what happened. It will answer all your questions," Clint replied. "I hope this person understands that we Ngobe have no international agreements about diplomats. They have no immunity here."

"Go for it!" Claberg cried.

"We met in the council room. These lawyers and diplomats presented the case that the pirate treasure on display here was the property of Spain. That, because Spain had originally paid a bunch of pirates to kill off a lot of the natives and steal their gold and jewelry. Because Spain paid for the murder and theft those things garnered through those acts were now and had been the property of Spain.

"Basilio ruled that this has to be the silliest piece of frivolity he has ever heard. Case was dismissed as being frivolous.

"Them's the facts. It's all recorded with video. What spin this guy wants to try to put on it is exactly that. Spin.

"Any other questions? Bear in mind that my

experience with the press hasn't always been good and note that I'm prone to get pissed when misquoted."

That got some laughter. Claberg yelled, "Thank you, Mr. President!" and they went for that beer.

Clint got the next call while enjoying the beer.

"Clint? Santo. Ramos is dead. He confronted Salvatore and was gunned down right there. The police came and no one would tell them what happened."

"A factor Capitan Ramos was instrumental in establishing himself. He was one who made the people feel it was dangerous to know anything about such actions.

"In other words he brought it on himself. Next case?

"Get through to the rest of the cops there that to mess with my friends in any way will bring me down on them like a plague. They'd _better_ understand that!

"My god! I sound obsequious to myself, but I mean it!"

"What's going on?" Claberg asked. Clint waved and chatted a minute more with Santo, then told Claberg it was a different matter. Corrupt thugs in Santiago killing each other off.

"I was into trying to do something about that bunch in Santiago, but it was brick wall after brick wall and a lot of harassment from the mob and their bought police.

"There aren't a lot of the police involved, Clint. A turkey named Ramos, who is probably who you were talking about, is the one who keeps the wall up and sees that cases don't turn up enough evidence to prosecute. Whatever this is, you won't get any evidence through to the court – that they would also buy off or intimidate."

"Not any more."

"Oh? Got caught?"

"Got dead. Salvatore's trying to put up a wall of his own."

"Ginoberto Salvatore? Maybe I should go to Santiago! He's the main one I was after!"

"And he's still alive and knocking off anyone who might be able to tag him with anything?"

"Right! Guess who would suddenly be on top of the list! It's probably better for us to stay out of it."

"If they don't go too far."

"Clint? Santo here. Emilio is in the hospital. Adames is dead. I am staying out of town now, but I want to go to Emilio."

Clint had gone to bed at eleven thirty. It was twelve twenty.

"I'll be there as fast as I can get there. I don't suppose I can use the chopper at this time of the night. Lay low until I can get there. They were warned about going too far.

"The chopper's waiting for me here. We can leave early enough to get there as soon as there's enough light to land."

He gave Santo instructions, then called Pedro Villares, the chopper pilot. Pedro said there were lights in Santiago. They could go now. He didn't need light to take off from a spot he knew.

Clint called Silvio back and told him what was happening, then grabbed his maleta and headed for the chopper. He was swearing colorfully as he got aboard. Pedro asked what was the problem and he said he had three perfectly good pistols in Quebrada Tula and he would need one of them in Santiago in a few minutes.

Pedro nodded and looked grim as he reached into the console to get a .357 Colt to hand to Clint.

"Your permit won't cover this, but I doubt the police here in Panamá would ask Clint Faraday to produce one anyhow."

He rummaged around and gave Clint a box of 24 bullets. He said he had another box somewhere if Clint needed them.

They landed in Santiago at 1:42AM. Clint had called Santo and asked about Emilio. He was in the regional hospital. There were sixty four Indios at the hospital. If anyone tried to get to Emilio they would have to go through them.

Clint and Pedro headed for the hospital. The Indios blocked them from going in until Pedro explained that this was Clint Faraday, Ngobe, here to teach that bunch of hoods a lesson about messing with his people.

An old man came to the door and greeted Clint. He was Nicanor Guerra, a friend from Rambala.

Clint was taken to the doctor on duty, who said Emilio was critical, but he would probably be alright. He had been shot in the shoulder, a couple of inches from a fatal wound. The slug had passed through. The danger was of infection, but Emilio was healthy and resistant.

Clint looked in, but Emilio was sedated. He went back to Pedro and Nica and asked what the police had done so far.

"Nothing. They said they couldn't find anyone who saw or heard anything," Nica reported.

"Did they recover the slug?"

"They didn't do anything."

"Do you know the exact location where he was shot?"

"Donaldo and Roberto do."

"I want ten of the people to go with me. I want that slug! We'll find it!"

Nica went out front where the police couldn't decide what to do. There would be a riot if they tried to make the people leave.

Clint explained that the people were not about to tolerate a bunch of thugs harming any of their brothers. They wouldn't do anything more than to make certain no one got to Emilio. They wanted to know who shot him. The police were refusing to investigate. That was going to require some explanation.

The officer in charge started to get huffy. Tito, a cop Clint had worked with in Las Tablas, whispered that this was Clint Faraday. He'd better check on what happens to anyone who tries anything crooked around him. He was a special officer with certification from Panamá City. Take note and have the sense to not try to obstruct him.

"Mr, Faraday? I'm Armando Cinches. I did not know it was you. I will cooperate in any way I can.

"A high police officer was shot earlier and we're short of experienced investigators, as a result."

"Ramos. He brought it on himself. Salvatore either shot him or ordered his death. That doesn't require much investigation.

"I want to know if Salvatore shot Emilio. If so, he will be tried on the comarca. He can't bribe or threaten his way out of anything there.

"If it wasn't him, we want whoever it was."

"But ... it was here he was shot, not on the

comarca!"

"And?"

Cinches looked around at the Indios. A couple more had just arrived. He shrugged. "I don't think I can stop this bunch from taking him to the comarca."

Clint shook his hand and went with the group Nica had selected to behind a hostel where the Indios stayed. It took more than an hour to find the slug. The search was minute and complete.

The slug had passed through Emilio. It was a hardened brass-jacketed slug and hadn't distorted much. It was lodged in a Novio tree trunk, which was why it was so hard to find.

"Forty. Probably a Glock. Not many others can use that bullet," Pedro suggested. "Not many brass jackets either. It shouldn't be hard to find the gun."

"If Ramos was shot with the same type slug, I'll find the piece of shit who fired them, I promise," Clint replied.

They went back to the hospital. Cinches had gone to the station. Nica had promised there would be no trouble started by the Indigenos, but there would be an immediate response to any provocation.

"I made it the word of Clint Faraday. I hope you will forgive that subterfuge."

"It's exactly what I would have said," Clint said. "I have to see if they have the slug that killed Ramos."

"Some of them. It was almost a shootout. If not, we will find the slugs fired toward Ramos. He fired a few himself."

Clint and Pedro went to the police station. Cinches checked the evidence and said they had two types of slugs that could be the ones that killed Ramos. Yes, one was a .40 brass jacket. The other was a .32 and may not have been fired at that time.

"Where will I find Salvatore?" Clint asked.

"Mr. Faraday, I beg you not to face him! He is a very dangerous person!"

"Does he carry a Glock Forty?"

There was a pause, then, "Yes. And he has special bullets."

"So you already know he killed Ramos and shot Emilio."

"Ramos, yes. Your friend, we don't know. We did not find the bullet."

"Did you try?"

"Yes, Mr. Faraday. We felt it was not in the area."

"It took us an hour with eleven of us searching, so I can believe that."

"Mr. Faraday, I do not want to place another

person at risk. I know from the information we have about you that you feel the same. That you will protect innocent bystanders.

"There was a man with Salvatore. A woman I will not identify saw them leaving the back alley where Ramos was killed. She could not clearly identify Salvatore, but described him. The other might have been a gringo. She heard them talking in English. She understands a little. The other said to Salvatore, 'That motherfucker hit me in the leg!'

"We are now looking for someone who speaks English who has a wound in the leg.

"We are investigating this, Mr. Faraday. Ramos isn't here to stop us anymore.

"To be quite honest with you, we did not bother to investigate Ramos too very much. We are investigating, quietly, any other incidents."

Clint shook his hand and said he would do what he could to try to stop some of these kinds of amateur mobsters.

"Tell anyone else who was into the corruption that I'm coming after them. Involving a Ngobe was going too far. If they kept it among their own select little group I would refuse to investigate myself when they killed each other off.

"I have to find what Emilio and Santo know. It's something they aren't aware they know. It's something without meaning to the Indios.

"They couldn't care less ... if....

"I wonder! Was that Freudian?"

"What? As is in the information about you, there are times when you make no sense, but you do get results."

Clint thought about some things. He suddenly asked, "Is Carlos Sargento Panamanian?"

"Sargento? I think perhaps ... a moment." He went to a file cabinet and searched through the folders. He pulled one out and studied it a moment.

"He is from Madrid. He has been here since he was a small child. His father was a diplomat. He has traveled to Spain four times. He became a citizen in eighty seven through application when he had been married to Leona Moreno Artez. He divorced her in twenty oh eight because she cannot bear children. He has been living in Brazil for four years.

"Moreno's father was a mobster himself. There is a note here that he was once incarcerated for two years for fraud. Is that pertinent?"

"To tell the truth, I don't know. It may be a coincidence about time and a statement a lawyer made yesterday. I don't want to believe that they're all in some idiotic scheme that won't work — but they didn't consider that the comarca law isn't the same ... and they always come from the money angle.

"This is ridiculous! Was this just to get me away from Buabidi? Are they so stupid they think they can pull off some scheme by getting me away where they would be dealing with Basilio and Silvio? Either one of them is more savvy than I am! Christ!"

"They want to get you away from the comarca? Why?" Pedro asked.

"Because they think I give orders there. I don't. I take orders there. I'm not a chief. The council holds almost absolute power so far as law goes.

"Armando, let it be known that involving any Indio in any way ever again will result in a few thousand of us coming here to clean this place of parasites and garbage!

"Pedro, back to Buabidi! Fast!

"Armando, tell Nica I said for him to be ready to move against Salvatore and a couple of people who will be named later.

"Caio!"

<u>*A Convoluted Mess*</u>

They came aground in Buabidi at just after three o'clock. Clint couldn't believe how fast things had happened.

As they came in Clint noted the limousine in front of the council house. That wasn't in the least unexpected. If he was right about what he now suspected it was inevitable.

He went to the hotel to put his maleta in his room. Silvio had arranged when the museum was built that a large part of the hotel was for the Ngobe. The rest could be used by anyone.

"Buabidi is the capital of the Ngobe Bugle comarca. The Ngobe people have conducted the necessary business of the comarca for decades here. The museum is new and will be bringing in many thousands of tourists. They will not be permitted to disrupt the comarca.. The museum will operate in ways that do not interfere with the realities of life. If it becomes necessary we will construct a large and very expensive hotel to serve the outsiders. The museum, like everything else here, is the property of the Ngobe. That includes the ways of life."

The argument of the others was, "We come here to spend our money. We should be given first preferences. After all, the Ngobe don't have the money unless we spend it here."

"We have the ship and treasures plus a life that requires no money. The value assessed of that ship, the treasures and the history is something close to forty billions of dollars. Your six million dollars per year that you will spend here is a pittance."

"That's the property of the government, not the people."

"The people are the government here. This is not a lip-service democracy."

"Well, we think you should do much more to accommodate the ones who bring in the money."

"Your life is all money. Ours is not. Most here do not want you or your money. If you can't abide by the rules here, go elsewhere."

"We'll see how long you can exist without our power and money!"

"Council declares you to be personas non gratas and demands your immediate removal from Ngobe land. You my not return. Should you do so you will be declared outlaw and treated as such."

"You can't do that!"

"I just did. Be off Ngobe land within the hour."

Clint remembered the exchange. It was carried

on TV. Three days of trying to reach an "accord" netted them nothing. Rojelio was chief of the council. It was fun watching an eighty nine year old Indio throwing a bunch of politicians from four countries off the comarca. It should have gotten through to this bunch, then, that a scheme using politics was dead before it started.

Clint went into the council room to find two lawyers, the former diplomat and another man Clint had seen several times in Panamá City. At the US Embassy. Silvio and Basilio were there, looking amused.

"Ah! Clinton! You are back here very quickly it would seem!" Basilio greeted. "Tyna called and said to remind you about the cloth. She said it was fifty-fifty you'd forgotten."

"To tell the truth, I had. I'll get it as soon as I leave. These ridiculous clowns aren't capable of understanding our people. Their diverting me to Santiago will result in a bunch of half-assed mobsters getting dead, I suppose. It'll serve for that, at least.

"Oh, Smithson, was it? One of your operatives was shot in the leg if they haven't reported that yet. Thank him for getting rid of Ramos. That will leave you and your crooked politics out in the cold – if you could say it's ever cold in Santiago.

"Has it gotten through to this gaggle of morons

that you can't be bought or intimidated yet, Silvio?"

"They are becoming boring. I am trying to decide how to handle them in what they would call a diplomatic manner. Typical crap."

"Why bother? Rojelio solved that problem a couple of years ago."

Basilio laughed. "It seems that your friend from the embassy has made some poorly veiled threats about what one stealth bomber could do here."

"What? Blow up the museum so no one gets anything?

"Shoot it down. You've proven you can with that deal when the Argentinians were trying to get the phosphate from over by the coast."

"Oh, come on! How would some ... the Indios shoot down a stealth bomber? I was just saying that we could use it to observe this place, not as a threat."

"Uh-huh," Basilio replied. "I'm too stupid to know what you were saying. I'd think the fact you can't understand a simple thing, such as the fact we don't play political games with a bunch of phony diplomats here, shows who's stupid.

"As to shooting down your big bad bomber, you might want to check with the scientists from your country who examined two planes we did shoot down. (Book 19: *A Moving Target*) You'll find that this bunch of ... Indios can and will protect ourselves from your killing machines.

"I agree with Clint about Rojelio's solution. I request that the rest of the council consider that solution."

"Maybe you'd better look at the realities of the world around you!" Smithson snarled. "Like it or not, the world operates on money! You'd better come into this century!"

"How diplomatic. Perhaps you'd better consider that we have the money and that our lifestyle is working very well, thank you, while yours are in constant turmoil," Silvio replied. "I wished to avoid taking strong steps, but am learning that they are the only way you will understand.

"Very well. If you pursue the course you've set you and the people of your countries on the list you provided will be expelled from the comarca and you will not be allowed to return. You can then explain to your people that you are the direct cause of that.

"Mr. Smithson, most of the gringos here are good people. Why your government insists upon using persons such as yourself has always been a mystery to me. I can now see it is because you have become decadent to the point money is all that is of concern to you. You think money gives you power.

"Perhaps it does. Outside."

"If you think I'm going to sit here and listen to some...!" Smithson started.

"Smithson! This is not some scripted movie where you will start a confrontation that ends up with you gaining anything!" the Spanish diplomat warned in English. "I'd advise that you silence yourself!"

"To which I would agree," Basilio replied, in English.

"Yes. Mr. Smithson tends to believe we are as ignorant as is he," Silvio said, also in English.

"I promise! You haven't heard the last of this!" Smithson yelled.

"Clint, please ask the guard squad to send some people here," Silvio requested. Clint went out front to call four of the museum guards over. He took them into the room where Smithson was arguing heatedly with the Spanish diplomat and his lawyers.

Silvio nodded and ordered, "Guard, escort Mr. Smithson to the border. He is not to return to the comarca. Ever. He is declared outlaw the moment he passes the border. Should he resist he is declared outlaw as of that moment. You may shoot him.

"Sr. Modesto, I ask that you please not conduct yourself in a manner that would make the same apply to you.

"The council rejects all points presented. The museum and all other things of the comarca are the property of the people, not of a few crooked politicians. Our people will not tolerate a corrupt crook on the council.

"Clint, I greatly fear we will need the weapon again. Is it possible your friend will grant its use under the same agreement as at Greenwater?"

"If the Ngobe are attacked, I guarantee it!"

"You say that you actually can shoot down such as the stealth bomber?" a lawyer asked.

"You didn't research that before you came here to make threats and attempt corrupt practices?" Basilio asked.

"It wasn't mentioned. If there is such a thing, we wouldn't be here, knowing of it," Modesto replied.

"There is," Clint said. "I'm going to Tula. I'll grab the cloth and have Pedro fly me home."

"Does the comarca pay for your use of that helicopter – or Panamá?" Modesto asked.

"Clint pays for it. He has many millions of dollars, personally. He does find it useful at times," Basilio said. "Clint, would there be room and would you allow me to return to Cusapín in the chopper?

"You see, I am a little corrupted by money and

ease."

"You'll get fat and lazy!" Clint shot back.

"Lazy? Maybe. Fat? Never!" They went out joking. Silvio looked at the lawyers and diplomat, who didn't seem to know what to do.

"You may report that the comarca will not make any deals to screw its people," Silvio announced. "Enjoy your stay, but please don't continue with this silliness."

"I think I respect you as much as I have ever respected anyone. I sometimes wish, deeply, that our diplomacy was as blunt and direct."

"Then it wouldn't be diplomacy. It would be truth. Ain't gonna happen!" Silvio returned.

"Agreed! Can I buy you a beer?" Modesto said, grinning. "We can talk about women and booze, no more so-called diplomacy. Not with you! It doesn't work!"

Ten seconds later the room was empty.

The chopper dropped Clint at his place outside of Quebrada Tula and continued on with Basilio for the Caribbean coast and Cusapín. Tyna came to hold Clint a long moment. He gave her the cloth and they went to the comfortable little house. The kids came home from school and they played a bit, then everyone took care of their responsibilities.

In the morning Clint went to work with the yuca. Nito went with Omar to fish. Nicole and Tyna went to the council house to sew some things for the comida house.

The following day Clint worked the cacao and coffee. He went home tired and satisfied.

He thought about those money people and shook his head. They had all kinds of luxury and ease and lacked a real purpose in life.

He was personally very wealthy, but worked with the other of his people. He had a place and a purpose that wasn't based in greed.

He thought about his life in the states and grimaced. It was a pointless existence there.

He thought about the differences in himself.

He was among the luckiest people in the world.

He was just getting up before sunrise the next day when he got another phone call. Things were getting serious in Santiago. Some diplomat from the US Embassy, or an agent or something, was dead.

Dead serious – again, Clint thought.

Clint stepped out of the chopper. Cinches was there to greet him and say there were now two dead people, supposedly from the US Embassy in Panamá City.

"And one has a gunshot wound in his left thigh. A thirty two, which is what Ramos carried. The hidden one."

"Name?"

"Edward Gaines, according to the passport he was carrying. His Texas driver's license said he was George Irvins. His Ohio driver's license said he was Earl G. Parkinson."

"Who was the other one?"

"James Smithson. That one will be legitimate."

"So. Now we're tied to Buabidi again. I don't have a clue as to what's going on. Why do the US and Spain want to get their hands on that pirate treasure so bad? What have we missed?

"Armando, none of this connects for some reason. It definitely has something to do with that ship and mobsters here and Spain and the US, among other more minor participants.

"I think I've made a big mistake in not reading

over what those people presented! I don't think it's really the treasure they're after!

"What could be ... I have to contact Silvio. He'll have the original demanda."

"You are back to making no sense, thus I know you will solve whatever it is you wish to solve.

"Armando, were those two shot with the same gun?"

"They weren't shot. They were killed with a knife. Quite expertly, which is why I'm sure it was not an Indio who killed them. The Indios would hack them up with dull machetes."

"I agree. They would also call me to explain why they did it."

They compared notes for a few minutes, then Clint went out to where he knew he wouldn't be overheard and used a throwaway cell phone to call Silvio.

"Silvio, can you fax me copies of the original demanda as presented by Modesto?"

"I can have Nilsa e-mail a scan," he replied. "I'm learning about this modern technology crap, you see."

Clint went to the hotel, got his laptop out and turned it on. He had a satellite connection. He was connected immediately.

It was thirty five minutes later when he got and e-mail with attachment. He opened it with his fax viewer and read through a lot of double-talk crap that never had a chance of passing the council. He found what he wanted hidden in a small clause four pages in.

... will retain all records from the vessel to be disbursed only by and/or with permission of Spain ...

What was in those records that would put both Spain and the USA in such a bad position?

That was hidden in a list of clauses about releasing information that may be discovered in future research.

Clint sat back. One thing was certain now. He wanted to spend whatever time it took to read every word on anything found on that ship!

Why this crap now? Why were two US agents killed? Was that connected?

When this went down the US was just being formed. They weren't getting along with Spain.

Clint called Silvio again. "Silvio, has Modesto or anyone else contacted you again?"

"No, but there is something strange here."

"What?"

"Someone has been trying to get into the vault that stores the papers."

"I doubt they can."

"I also. It makes me wonder about what is in that vault."

"Me, too. I'll try to get there tomorrow. We can try to find it first. I have to find what Emilio knows."

"Emilio? In the hospital? He is the only one who was attacked. He knows something he is not aware he knows. I see."

"Or someone else thinks he does."

They chatted a minute more, then Clint headed for the hospital. Emilio was recovering very well and Clint would be the only one, other than Santo, who would be allowed to speak with him. He was led to a room with several Indios in the hallway. There was only one entrance to the room.

Emilio had a couple of antibiotic drips or something attached, but was alert.

"Clint, I don't understand why they want to kill me. I do not know what is happening."

"Emilio, it has something to do with the pirate ship in Buabidi. What do you know about it?"

"I was there when it was brought in and worked sometimes with a crew to make the safe vaults. I helped bring many of the things from the ship to the vaults. It was in English so I didn't know much of it."

"Who, here, did you tell about that?"

"Only some bar talk. I told them I didn't read any of it because it was in English. It is why I can't understand why Spain would want anything because it wasn't a Spanish ship, then Donny said it had a lot of things on it that was taken from Spanish ships."

"Did this Donny person ask anything specific? I mean, about a certain place or time or paper or anything."

"Well, I remember ... one time I said there was something about St. Augustine where the ship was, but that seemed strange because I didn't know that the ship ever went across out of the Caribbean except outside of Cuba and up to Charleston, which I know is in the United States.

"It was in an old book I was carrying that fell out of the crate. I put the paper back."

"I think maybe that paper is as important to some people as any paper that was every written. I can't see what difference it could make now. It was more than a hundred eighty years ago!"

They talked for awhile, but that was the only definite thing Emilio remembered that could possibly be a connection.

"Who is Donny?" Clint asked.

"He was just some Canadian fellow who was here because of the hydroelectric project. We were talking in a bar. He didn't know anything about the place and came in because it was there. He seemed to get along well with the Indigenos and said it was a bad thing for the government to treat us the way the government is treating us."

Was all this because of some chance encounter in a bar? Did someone who knew someone else mention it in passing? Did someone add two and two and get eighty seven point four?

Stranger things had happened.

Did Donny know a jerk at the US Embassy and mention he'd met an Indio who read a paper from the old pirate ship in Buabidi? A paper that said there was a connection with pirates from Spain and pirates from St. Augustine?

Did Francisco, the pirate who had the ship and who established a village in Panamá, take the ship from a pirate sponsored by someone in the US?

It didn't make much sense. There had to be more. What had happened back then that could affect anyone now?

Clint decided he was going back to Buabidi. Emilio described the book. It was a book of sea maps with pages of charts and dotted lines and navigational information.

Clint called Tyna and talked about a lot of things, then called Pedro to take him to Buabidi. He called Silvio to say he was coming. They would go directly to that vault.

Clint felt the paper Emilio saw was one of several. It would be the combination that sealed that deal!

It was just getting dark in Buabidi when they landed. Clint went to the hotel, then to talk with Silvio. They would meet in the morning and go to the storage vault together. Clint was exhausted and would miss too much tonight.

He had a good meal, caught up his e-mail and messages, called Judi Lum, his neighbor and close friend in Bocas Town, chatted with Dave, the nutty musician/botanist/ author friend who had a weapon the Indios had used to stop a takeover of some of their land, then sacked out. He slept nearly nine hours, which was extreme for him.

At six thirty in the morning he went with Silvio to the museum. They went to the vault and found the two large crates of books and papers from the ship. Historians were given access to part of it, but the descendants of the pirates first went through to see what they could find about their ancestors.

Four and a quarter hours later Silvio called that he had found the book Emilio spoke of. There were several papers inserted between the pages. It was an old navigational book that was added to when a new area was explored. The papers were actually log pages that were secreted in an old book no one would read.

Silvio looked over the first one and handed it to Clint:

July 13, 1797

Stopped island south of peninsula of Florida. Nothing there. Proceed NNE by N.

Stopped at settlement St. Augustine. Fired on by cannon. Remained standing offshore until dory approached. Lt. Oswald Fournier says they were attacked in past. Will work deal for protection. Cpt. Melendez there. From Colombia. Has deal for protection down there to transport gold from Colombia to here or to Charleston Harbour. Melendez will identify vessels to attack. Spain will buy gold or trade for whatever else. Cpt. Miller of the new country growing here will guarantee cooperation of this country as they wish to establish regular trade routes with England and Holland as well as Spain and Portugal. It is a secret agreement among the merchants in those countries. Jacob Sterling will be moderator and will control most phases.

Will consider.

A deal with the enemy, several of them, to rape South America? It was only history. Why all this crap now?

Where had he heard of Jacob Sterling?

Next page:

September 6, 1798

Returned from Charleston Harbour. Delivered ton + gold and a chest with sixty four pounds of emeralds and sapphires in gold settings and some silver bars. Fur person from Canada seems to be backing part of it. I don't like it with Fournier and another Frenchman involved. You can't trust them. He talks about Sterling. Sterling talks about Fournier. Somebody said Germans behind it all. They aren't regular Germans. I don't know what they mean. I'm keeping my oars in the water with these people.

Germans, but not regular Germans?

Last page:

February 19, 1800

Terrible weather today. Was going to deliver cargo St. Augustine. Attacked. Believe Melendez and Stromm were behind it. Won't deliver cargo. Won't contact them. The Prussians have ruined the chances of this working. On my own. Trouble with crew because of captive. Claims to be royalty. Spain. Will offload cargo when can. Take captive to Dominica. For ransom.

There was another page somewhere. It would be a page that affected the royal lineage of Spain. Clint was remembering a little bit about a Jacob Sterling. He had freed a son of a royal family in Spain. There was some question or another about it. Some claimed he was a fraud.

It didn't actually affect the royal lineage. The heir didn't ever get to the point where he was king. A closer relative became king, though it looked for a short while like he would have inherited the throne.

What did that have to do with anything now?

"Silvio, there's another page somewhere. There has to be. This mess doesn't mean anything without it."

"I think that perhaps this piece written on the reverse of a page may be what you seek?" Silvio showed Clint the note. It was on the back of the last page filled out in the log.

Feb 21 – Delivered captive. He was murdered on the dock. Believe it was Stromm. Nobody else that big here. Stromm later in bar with person who looked like captive. Crew close to mutiny. No ransom. Will sail for Colombia now.

"This is in the handwriting of one before the crew who came here," Silvio said. "You can compare. They are not alike. We have records where our people took over. Clint, that imposter never became king. Why are they so concerned about it now? Someone else inherited the throne."

"I believe inheritance may have a lot to do with it. I have to get to the net to research this, but I'm remembering a bit more. I read it fifteen or twenty years ago. It's not clear anymore."

They carefully sealed the log with its inserts in the vault. Clint made photocopies of everything to take with him. He went to the hotel and got his laptop to do some serious research of things that happened more than two hundred years before.

"What happened according to what I can find is that the question of the heir was so strong they made a ruling about future inheritance for twelve generations. All the holdings of the heir were in a trust. The several since have been wastrels and worse, but a few were excellent in business. A lot of the business was crooked, but they made a lot of millions of dollars that they live on from the interest. The way the decree was worded, proof that Esteban was not Esteban means the fortune reverts to Spain.

"This is convincing proof that Esteban wasn't Esteban. From what I can find, four families now will lose more than fifty million Euros in cash and hundreds of millions in businesses. It's really a weird situation. Coming from me, that's really *weird*! Some other things have been weird, but this political maneuvering over money gets the prize. I think the whole family is genetically criminal. You should read about some of the things they've done. Everything from mafia-like practices to sadistic monsters.

"I doubt the decree will hold up, but it should."

"So all they wanted was to get that one paper. They are powerful enough to get Spain and the

USA to aid them?" Silvio asked.

"If you saw a couple of the names of their close relatives, you'd understand in an instant. They're money-obsessed sick people who don't care *how* they get money, just *that* they get it. They have a talent to seem good, honest people. They're genetic sociopaths. They project emotions, but don't actually feel anything. I've come across a lot of those in my life. Several here in Panamá. There was one group who were killing each other off for the sole purpose of feeling something – and never did. Most of them seemed to be smart and friendly. (Book 9: *Follow the Blood*)

"I'll have to go to Santiago again. I don't know how that bunch are involved. I don't really know how I got involved.

"I wonder!"

"What?"

"I have to get some information with the computer. That original pirate was *here*, not in Spain.

"Maybe ... Jacob Sterling. Was he actually Joshua Silvers?"

"Who was?

"This is fascinating – and I have no concept of what is going on!"

"I came across a lot of names while tracing the lineage of that royal heir. A first cousin was Estrella Cuestras Vega or something such who married ... what was the name? Francis Silvers? The son was named Joshua Silvers. He was never mentioned again in that lineage. The time was right. I want to look at the data about others in that branch of the family."

"But there isn't anything to tell you about why you were brought into it. I admit it has stopped making sense to me altogether."

Clint went back to the computer to study some old records from minor history works that were scanned and put on the net. There were thousands of such works, of interest only to historians. There was information about millions of people that was there if you know how to find it. Clint was good at that.

He finally sat back to think, then went back to list a long sheet of family lineage. He found what he half-expected. It left him with more questions than answers. The basic question was: Why? Why was Clint Faraday involved in this idiocy?

It had to be because a woman named Faith Richards was a member of that family. She was exactly that type of sociopath. She was one of the group who were a collection of sociopaths who made a game of killing each other off.

About time to head for Santiago and wrap this mess up!

<u>*Wrapping It Up*</u>

Clint took a bus this time. He wasn't in such a hurry. He relaxed a little on the trip and studied what he had found. He went to other sites on his laptop to add little connecting details. He had the story pretty well laid out when he got off the bus in Santiago. He went directly to the hospital to chat awhile with Emilio, Santo and the other Indios there. Emilio could go home in two more days.

He went to the police station and waited until Cinches came back from an arrest of a man and woman who were running a scam. They had been paying Ramos to protect them. Cinches was now tracing all such deals he could and was making arrests. A few people had decided to move to other places.

Three more hoods had killed each other off, but the one causing it all was sitting back watching it. Clint wondered if he felt anything when somebody killed somebody else because he set them up. He doubted it.

The next stop was at the corregidor to get the warrants to bring the people he wanted to have together brought in. Cinches was nervous about some of them. Clint said they could be told that this was not about any action against them. It was to show them how they had been set up. Ramos had hidden their part so well that they wouldn't have any evidence against them – which was why it was inordinately stupid to kill him. Cinches would act against them if they did anything more, so take note and let discretion rule in the future.

They would have their little yakking session in the corregidor's office at nine in the morning.

Clint spent the rest of the day with his friends and sacked out about midnight, after spending an hour and a half on the phone with his family.

Clint looked around the room. The four major hoods still around in Santiago and the people who drew them all into this thing. Cinches made a short speech that suggested the past of certain of them could be forgotten, but only so long as they didn't resume their old activities. They had made enough to be quite comfortable. Jail wasn't comfortable.

Carlos Sargento said he didn't have a clue as to why he was there. He didn't have anything in his past that concerned the police in Santiago.

"I believe you would much prefer that things that you have done here would only concern my department," Cinches fired back. "It concerns others in this room. Very deeply.

"I will now request that Clint Faraday take charge of this gathering and that he makes it as short as he can. I have work to do."

Clint went to stand in front of them. He looked around and noted the amused look on Sargento's face. Knowing what he did, he knew it was a practiced pose, no more.

Why not take that look off his face?

"Oh, Carlos! Tell Faith I said hello if you ever get to the states to see her again."

A flicker of ... something ... went across his face. He grinned. "Faith?"

"Your cousin, who turned you onto me and Panamá.

"The reason we're here in this group is because Carlos set you up to knock each other off. It was mostly to divert me from what was happening in Buabidi. He wanted to be able to steal four sheets of paper – well, only one of them meant anything without the others.

"I don't think he really cares even about that. If the trust is actually reverted to Spain it will cost Carlos and family a few hundred million. I don't believe they will really care. They're all genetic sociopaths and don't really feel anything."

Carlos grinned and nodded. "It really doesn't

mean anything. Nothing does. I'll still have a couple of million that I'll waste trying to discover what is lost in me that all of you, well, except Charlie and Jorge, here, have.

"Charlie and Jorge are people Faith introduced me to. They're deficient in the same way as Faith and me.

"Some in the family might miss the money, but I really think it's been much too long. The trust conditions won't apply anymore.

"Faith always said you were able to make life interesting for a few minutes. I decided to see if that was true. She said she would be totally in love with you if she could feel anything at all.

"I'm not going to deny anything. I didn't do anything other than show these types that they were fools to trust each other for ten seconds. I don't feel anything, they do. They are deficient in much more serious ways than am I. They feel, yet they do the things they do. I can't understand it. I would feel the horror I can fake if I could feel.

"I once thought it was a thing brought on by incidences in my past, but it is a very solid and definite part of everyone in my family, so it has to be genetic. Uncle George is the weird one in the family. He does feel. He knows horror at what the family is. He can be unhappy while I can't even have that.

"It is why I have no children and won't. They would be deficient in the ways I am.

"Well, Clint! I have been honest with you, so took some of the wind from your sails!"

"You have? How?" Clint asked.

Carlos cocked his head to the side, then grinned again. "You were going to expose me for what I am and get these worthless pieces of shit to get rid of me for you. It's how you operate. I have to admit I find that rather intelligent. They are here now because they can control the law so well."

"No," Clint replied, shaking his head. "I haven't exposed anything. You did. All I wanted to do is make it clear that no more of my people are to be used in such a way. I won't have these, as you say, pieces of shit, knocked over by each other and you in that case. I'll handle it. I am the law, by agreement.

"I want to make it plain that I will handle any or all of you in a simple way. You will be charged and taken to the comarca to be tried by the people you have used. There is already an agreement in place for that. It would be a matter of taking one or two of you to the comarca or of one or two thousand of my people coming here to get you."

"That was the thing that scared the piss out of me with you," Salvatore said. "I heard you tell Ramos you would bring the Indios here, so many the army couldn't stop you.

"It was Smithson who set that up where your friend was shot. I told him that would be stupid beyond idiocy, but he said it was the way to get you involved that couldn't fail.

"I never knew why he wanted you to come here. He said it was so you wouldn't be somewhere else.

"You went back to Buabidi anyhow. He came here with that chulo to shut me up. He wanted to make sure you would never know he was the one who was doing that. It was them or me. I'm here. No apologies for killing someone who was trying to kill me!"

"Carlos, why was he involved? He wasn't part of the family," Clint asked.

"He was there and he was someone who tended to treat others like insects. He had a very high opinion of himself, without basis. He often used people, then discarded them. I used him, then discarded him.

"As you would say, turn about is fair play."

Clint nodded. "I can accept that, but there was something more involved. Blackmail?"

He laughed. "You are very intelligent. It was more a matter of him trying to shake down the wrong people. We tend to resent that. I live my life, such as it is, on an accounts sheet. I owe people, they owe me. Him, I paid off a debt. Now I am the one owed."

"That works in it's own sorta odd way," Clint replied. "Anyone else have any questions?"

"Yes, Clint," Santo said. "Why was Emilio shot? I don't understand."

"That was Smithson," Salvatore answered. "He wanted an Indio, preferably Ngobe, hurt. He was never meant to be killed, I swear. I would have not done that. He moved at the wrong time or the wound would have been less. In the arm, not the shoulder.

"Emilio had spoken with someone in a bar. He knew about the ship. Clint is involved with the ship. He would come.

"I imagine Clint has sought to find why your friend was shot. It didn't lead anywhere because it was only a convenient way he could ... it led somewhere?"

"It led to us being here in this room right now," Clint replied. "It led to finding four sheets of paper."

"My god!" Carlos exclaimed. "I just felt something! It was something like ... excitement? I don't know.

"This is a comedy. I think I felt ... fun?

"A man is shot for the reason of distracting you from the fact there is a report in Buabidi that some in the family feel must be destroyed. You would probably have never found the papers if that shooting didn't make you concentrate on the reason the man was shot! Distracting you from it led you to it!

"Four expert thieves tried to get to those papers, but found it was not possible. They would never have been found, except they were spoken of by the shot man. It is a circle within a circle. When found, the papers won't mean anything except to historians. That old condition of trust can't be honored after twenty one years by Spanish law! It has been two hundred!

"Hee-hee! This is ... I think that was the first time in my life I laughed because of something I feel, not as an act, a facade!

"Faith was right! You made me feel something for a minute! It was worth it!"

"I didn't make you feel anything. The situation did. It really is a silly kind of comedy. If it wasn't for the fact Emilio was hurt I think I could enjoy it!" Clint said.

"Emilio will enjoy it," Santo said. "It really is funny in a bad sort of way."

"I can't see anything funny about it!" Salvatore snapped.

"Yes. It also results in your knowing you must change your ways while you do not know another way," Cinches accused. "I find that refreshing!

"Shall we all pretend we are civilized people and agree to, at least, *try* to live a better life?"

"You sound obsequious," Carlos fired back. "I like the idea, but you didn't have to say it in such an effete way!"

"I agree with that!" Salvatore cried. "You really went too far with that!"

Cinches laughed and gave them all the finger. They started a silly joke session and went away, not friends by any wild stretch, but not quite the same degree of enemies. Carlos was going back to Brazil, Cinches was going back to the station, Santo was going to the hospital.

Clint was going home.

<u>*Peace*</u>

Clint tousled Nito's hair. Nito was laying against him in the large hammock on the porch of the Quebrada Tula place. Nicole brought some banana pineapple chicha from the kitchen, Tyna went out to watch the sunrise from the porch.

A couple of the white-faced monkeys that were almost pets came to beg a banana or two from Tyna. Four or six noisy green parrots stopped for a minute in the breadfruit tree, then flew on.

Nicole sat at the computer to chat with friends all over the world with Skype. Nito said he was going to the garden to get rid of the bugs that came in the night to chew up the vegetables. He climbed out of the hammock and went in to put on some clothes.

Nicole said that Clint had an e-mail from someone called Armando Cinches. Clint took the laptop on the table and turned it on. He brought up his e-mail and deleted the fourteen spams, then opened the one from Armando.

Clint, dear friend – I felt you might have interest in the resolution of the case where Carlos

Sargento, of Brazil, caused the area of Santiago to experience much less organized criminality. He has sent me an e-mail, and to you, also, I would think. He and his friends will not again come to Panamá, for which I am relieved.

The court here has ruled that he committed no crime. He even prevented much future crime.

He is a strange person. I hope that he finds peace.

I also hope you will again come to Santiago. Life is more exciting when you are here. I remain your friend, always, Armando

Clint smiled. Carlos would never find peace, but he would never find anything else so maybe it would translate to something such.

There really was an e-mail from Carlos.

Greetings, Clint — I am home, as much as I can be. It is tranquil here. We are well and the courts have ruled that the terms of the trust were over one hundred forty six years ago and that Spain may claim nothing. I have no least idea where they arrived at that figure.

Faith will send you an e-mail. I gave her your address. She says I must credit her for arranging that I feel something for a minute. I do not yet know if that was a curse or a blessing. I will, quite probably, not feel again.

I wish to say that you have given me much. I

thank you. I wish you happiness – Carlos S.

Maybe he wasn't so bad. Certainly not nearly so bad as that group Faith had been part of.

He went down the list. There was an e-mail from believings _2012_pn.

Hi, Clint – Hope you remember me in less than distaste. Carlos found two minutes of feeling something and, unlike me, enjoyed it.

As you probably know, our little game group has dissipated until there are only three of us who communicate with one another now. That would probably be sad, if I could be sad.

Keep up the good work. If respect could be called a feeling, you make me feel that.

Good future – Faith

Well, that turned out better than he thought would be possible.

He turned off the computer. He didn't see any other messages he cared to read for the moment.

Nito came in to say there weren't many bugs today. The zucchini was ready for some of that Turkish pizza he made. He was going to help the council with the water tank Clint bought for the council house. It would be filtered water so would be safer for that. Clint had shown him how to do the work when he put in their own new tank.

Ten years old and already acting civil engineer! Clint thought.

Nicole said she was going to help at the school. There was no school today and she was good with numbers so would help list the things they had and what they needed. Clint said that was, "Taking inventory."

Tyna came to lay with him in the hammock. She was going to hang around the house with him today. They deserved one day a month to just be lazy slobs.

Clint sighed happily and cuddled with Tyna. After about an hour he had to move to be doing something. He wasn't made to just laze around anywhere, even for one day. Neither was Tyna.

"I think I'll dig out a spot by the stream for sugar cane," he said. "We have to move it. It's used up the soil where it is now. That's the only bad thing about sugar cane."

"I think I'll grind enough corn for a couple of months," Tyna said. "I've kept putting it off, but it has to be done."

They teased for a few minutes. Clint sighed again and kissed Tyna's beautiful long shiny black hair.

This was peace. It was a personal peace.

It was something no one in a city could ever know.

C. D. Moulton's works are available on most major outlets as printed or e-books. CD writes the CD Grimes, PI, mysteries, the Det. Lt. Nick Storie mysteries, the Clint Faraday mysteries, the Flight of the Maita science fiction series, books on orchid culture and many others of many types. Mystery, adventure, intrigue, science fiction, humor, fantasy, paranormal, mild erotica, and factual.